A Valentine
For Cousin Archie

by Barbara Williams
illustrated by Kay Chorao

E. P. Dutton   New York

Text copyright © 1981 by Barbara Williams
Illustrations copyright © 1981 by Kay Sproat Chorao

Library of Congress Cataloging in Publication Data

Williams, Barbara.   A valentine for Cousin Archie.

SUMMARY: Responding to the anonymous valentine
he receives, Cousin Archie sets off a whole chain
of valentine giving.
[1. St. Valentine's Day—Fiction.   2. Animals—Fiction]
I. Chorao, Kay.   II. Title.
PZ7.W65587Val [E]   80-181   ISBN: 0-525-41930-6

Published in the United States by E. P. Dutton, a Division
of Elsevier-Dutton Publishing Company, Inc., New York

Published simultaneously in Canada by Clarke,
Irwin & Company Limited, Toronto and Vancouver

Editor: Ann Durell   Designer: Stacie Rogoff

Printed in the U.S.A.   First Edition
10 9 8 7 6 5 4 3 2 1

This valentine goes to
Marolyn and John Siddoway,
with love.

This valentine goes to Elizabeth Forsberg

E. E.
B. W.

Barbara Milbain

"Yoohoo, Cousin Archie!" called Chester Chipmunk. "YOOHOO!"

"Goodness, Chester," said Cousin Archie. "What on earth are you bellowing for?"

"I'm delivering my valentines," said Chester. "I thought you might want to come with me."

"Heavens, Chester! In this blizzard? My lumbago would punish me for months!"

"It's not a blizzard, Cousin Archie," said Chester. "It's downy snowflakes. Anyway, if you fill a thermos with that nice hot pecan tea I can smell, we won't get cold at all."

"You must smell burned pecan pie,"
said Cousin Archie. "I wanted to bake you
a pecan pie for Valentine's Day, Chester. But
every time I try to bake pecan pie, I burn it."

"That's all right, Cousin Archie," said
Chester. "It's the thought that counts."

Cousin Archie hobbled to the stove
and poured himself a cup of nice hot
pecan tea.

"Hmmmpf!" he said to himself. "Chester
is off delivering valentines to strangers,
and he didn't even have one for his closest
flesh-and-blood relative."

Just then a cold gust of wind sent
tingles down Cousin Archie's neck. He
rushed to shut the door that had been
left ajar.

"Well, well." He picked up a piece of paper lying on the doorstep. "Chester left me a valentine after all."

But then his smile turned to a frown. This was the sissiest love note that any Chipmunk in the entire forest had ever sent. The valentine said,

I
PINE
TO
BE
ARCHIE'S

SWEET
TOOTSIE

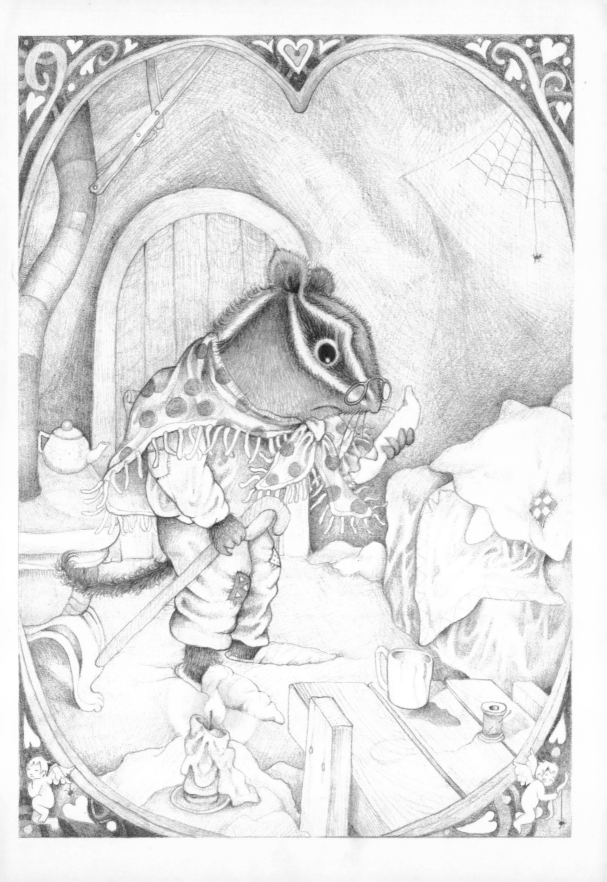

Furthermore, Cousin Archie could
smell a sweet odor coming from the
valentine. *Sniff,* went Cousin Archie.
Sniff, sniff, sniff. "Goodness!" he thought.
"Chester has even put perfume on this
silly valentine. The poor boy has gone
huckleberries. What will become of me
now that my very closest relative has
gone huckleberries?"

And Cousin Archie felt so sorry for
himself that he got a hot towel for his
forehead and lay down in bed.

Then a new thought came to him.
"What makes me so sure Chester sent me
that valentine? Maybe a lady admirer sent
it. Of course! That dainty kind of perfume
is just the sort that the Widow Cottontail
would use. Well!"

Cousin Archie sprang from bed and
gathered up some paper, some scissors,
a pen, and took the red satin ribbon from
around the bunch of holly that Chester
had given him for Christmas. He whistled
as he worked, and when he was through he
had a beautiful valentine. It said,

WIDOW
COTTONTAIL,
YOUR
TOOTSIE
PINES
TOO

   "Not bad. Not bad at all," thought Cousin
Archie. "I wish I could see the dainty Widow
Cottontail's face when she reads this."

"Dear me," said the Widow Cottontail reading her valentine. "That Aunt Geraldine of yours never could spell. And she's always getting everything else mixed up, too."

"Why do you say that, Mama?" asked Brunhilda.

"She misspelled $Y\text{-}O\text{-}U\text{-}'\text{-}R\text{-}E$ on this valentine. And she calls me 'Tootsie Pines.' Well, I happen to know there are no such trees as tootsie pines. There are Japanese pines and Austrian pines and ponderosa pines and Scotch pines. But there are no such trees as—"

"Let me see the valentine, Mama. Oh, Mama. Aunt Geraldine didn't send this."

"Of course she did," said the Widow Cottontail. "There are only two people in the whole world who ever send me valentines—Chester Chipmunk and your Aunt Geraldine. And Chester has already come by this morning."

"But Mama," said Brunhilda, "Aunt Geraldine doesn't call you 'Widow Cottontail.' She calls you 'Esmeralda.' I think a gentleman friend sent you this valentine."

"Tee hee," said the Widow Cottontail. "I wonder if it could have been Oswald Opossum. He winked at me when I walked underneath him yesterday, but I thought he just had a twitch in his eye."

"Oh, Mama! How exciting! You have a valentine from Oswald Opossum!"

"Dear me," said the Widow Cottontail. "Doesn't Oswald Opossum know there are no such trees as tootsie pines? He should know more about trees than anyone in these whole woods. He's always hanging by his tail from a tree."

"I don't think Oswald is talking about trees, Mama. I think this is a love message in code."

"Tee hee. Do you really? Well, why doesn't
he say what he means? Dear me, I wish he'd
stop hinting and say what he means."

"I have an idea, Mama. You send him a
valentine and ask him what he means. I'll
help you make it. I have some lace doilies
left over from the valentines I made for my
friends. And you can use the red ribbon
from the valentine he gave you."

The Widow Cottontail and Brunhilda
sang together as they worked, and when they
were through, they had a beautiful valentine.
It said,

DEAR VALENTINE,
GIVE ME
A BETTER HINT.
WHAT
DO YOU MEAN?

"Well, it's about time!" cried Oswald Opossum as he read his valentine. "I've been hinting to Mrs. Woodchuck all winter that I'd like some of her wonderful crabgrass stew. This time I'll give her a hint that she'll be sure to understand." So he gathered up some crabgrass he'd saved in his tree house and tied it up with the red satin ribbon from his valentine.

"Oh that Chester Chipmunk is such a
darling!" said Mrs. Woodchuck as she untied
the ribbon from her crabgrass.

"Mmmp," said Aaron Woodchuck, who
was eating a piece of taffy he had received
for a valentine.

"Imagine Chester's doing a sweet thing
like this!" said Mrs. Woodchuck.

"Mmmp," said Aaron.

"When he came over this morning
to deliver his valentine, I told him I was
out of crabgrass. So that dear thing has
gone off and found some for me. And
look at the pretty ribbon he tied it with.
I'll have to bake him one of his favorite
pecan pies to let him know how grateful
I am."

"Mmmp," said Aaron.

"Oooh." sighed Chester Chipmunk,
rubbing his stomach. "That was the most
delectable pie I've ever eaten. It's just like
Cousin Archie to pretend he burned my
valentine pie."

"Well, I'll show him that I'm on to his secret by using the red ribbon he tied around my pie to wrap up the valentine I'm giving him." And Chester sang happily as he got Cousin Archie's valentine present ready.

"Yoohoo, Cousin Archie!" Chester called. "YOOHOO!"

"Goodness, Chester," said Cousin Archie. "Are you still bellowing?"

"I just wanted to give you your valentine, Cousin Archie."

"Hmmmpf," said Cousin Archie. "I was wondering if you had saved any valentines for your flesh-and-blood relatives or if you had given them all to strangers."

"Oh, I didn't get a regular valentine for you, Cousin Archie. I knew you would think that valentines with ribbons and lace were for sissies, so I bought you something special. I bought you a hot water bottle for your lumbago."

"Thank you, Chester. Since I already have a *real* valentine from a lady admirer and don't need any more from you, a hot water bottle will come in very handy."

"Oh, Cousin Archie," cried Chester. "Why did you hang my shopping list on your wall?"

"Don't be silly, Chester. That isn't your shopping list. That's my valentine from a lady admirer. Smell the perfume."

Sniff, went Chester. *Sniff, sniff, sniff.* "Just what I thought. Insect repellent."

"Insect repellent!" exclaimed Cousin Archie. "How dare you call perfume from a lady admirer insect repellent!"

"But it *is* insect repellent, Cousin Archie. I spilled it myself on the way home from the store. See, here's the other half of the shopping list I tore up." And Chester unfolded a piece of paper and held it next to the one on the wall. Together they said,

SHOPPING LIST:

I NSECT REPELLENT
PINE APPLE
TO MATOES
BE ANS
ARCHIE'S HOT WATER
BOTTLE
SWEET POTATOES
TOOTSIE ROLLS

"Hmmmpf," said Cousin Archie, studying
the list. "Hmmmpf," he said again. "Well,
don't stand there feeling sorry for me just
because I didn't get any sissy valentines. Help
me fill my hot water bottle!"